PePPa the Mermaid

One afternoon, Peppa and Rebecca Rabbit were playing mermaids. "Aren't mermaids amazing, Rebecca?" said Peppa. "I'd love to have a shiny tail and swim underwater every day!" Peppa pretended to swim around the room, swishing her imaginary tail.

"Peppa!" called Daddy Pig. "Time for lunch."

At lunch, Peppa couldn't stop talking about mermaids.
"Mermaids only eat starfish-shaped sandwiches," she said.
"Mermaids can swim and dance at the same time!"

"Let's have an under-the-sea party!" said Rebecca.
"Yes!" cheered Peppa. "I can dress up as a mermaid!"
"Lovely idea," said Mummy Pig. "We can have it this Sunday."

Peppa and Rebecca made some under-the-sea party invitations.
"Very shiny," said Daddy Pig.
"Just like mermaids' tails!" said Peppa.

The next day, Peppa handed out the invitations.
"I'm having a mermaid under-the-sea party tomorrow," she told
everyone at playgroup. "It's going to have a beach, a disco and
an underwater tea party with starfish-shaped sandwiches!"

That night, Peppa was very excited.
"I've told everyone there's going to be a beach, a disco and starfish-shaped sandwiches at my party tomorrow."
"The party isn't tomorrow, Peppa. It's on Sunday," said Mummy Pig. "You'll have to wait one more day."

"But I told everyone the party was *tomorrow*," said Peppa.
She pulled out an invitation from under her pillow . . .

"Oh no," said Mummy Pig, looking at the invitation.
"We forgot to put the date on the invitations!"
"Well, we'll just have to do what we can for tomorrow, then,"
said Daddy Pig, smiling.

"Don't worry, Peppa," said Mummy Pig.
"We'll sort something out. Now get some sleep,
and we'll see you in the morning."

Mummy and Daddy Pig raced downstairs to do some research on the family computer.
"Now, let's see what we can find," said Daddy Pig.

Tap, tap, tap!

The computer screen filled with lots of amazing ideas for an under-the-sea party.
"Those look great, Daddy Pig!" said Mummy Pig.
"But how are we going to do them all for tomorrow?"

Daddy Pig thought hard. "Hmmm. I'm not sure," he said, yawning.
"I am a little bit tired. Maybe we should get some help?"
"Yes," agreed Mummy Pig. "What about that big red button?"

"Miss Rabbit – Emergency Party Planner
and Entertainer Extraordinaire," Daddy Pig read.

"Perfect," said Daddy Pig.
He pressed the big red button . . .

Just then, there was a knock at the door.
"Miss Rabbit – Emergency Party Planner and
Entertainer Extraordinaire," said Miss Rabbit.
"I hear you are in need of an under-the-sea party?"

"Yes," said Daddy Pig, telling Miss Rabbit
their ideas. "For tomorrow!"
"No problem," said Miss Rabbit.
"You go to bed. I've got this!"

In the morning, Peppa and her family woke up and walked downstairs. When they reached the living room, they were amazed. Their house had been transformed into an underwater wonderland!

"Look, George, there's a beach!" gasped Peppa. "And waves!"
"Wow!" said Daddy Pig. "The living room looks just
like the Great Barrier Reef from our trip to Australia!"

Peppa found some costumes hanging up.
"Ooooh!" she squealed in delight.
"This mermaid costume has the
shiniest tail I have ever seen!"

Mummy and Daddy Pig went into the kitchen
and looked in the fridge. It was full of delicious food.
"Miss Rabbit is amazing!" said Daddy Pig.
"She really is," agreed Mummy Pig.

That afternoon, Peppa and George's friends arrived.
They were all dressed in their underwater costumes.
"Hello!" said Peppa, swimming up to greet them.
"I'm Peppa the mermaid and this is George the crab.
Welcome to our under-the-sea home!"
"WOW!" everyone gasped.

After everyone had arrived, Miss Rabbit swam
into the room. "Hello, sea creatures," she began.
"It's time for your underwater adventure!"
"Hooray!" cheered Peppa and her friends.

First, Miss Rabbit asked the children to wiggle their toes in the sand.

"Oooh, it feels all tickly!" said Peppa.

Next, Miss Rabbit handed out seashells. "Put the shells to your ears and tell me what you can hear."
"The sea!" shouted all the children.

Then Miss Rabbit gave them some smelly toy fish.
"Take a good sniff. What can you smell?"
"Erghhh!" shouted the children. "Fishy!"
"Well, we are at the seaside!" said Miss Rabbit.

"Now, sea creatures," said Miss Rabbit,
"are you ready to dive down to the bottom
of the ocean for an underwater tea party?"
"YES!" shouted the children.

After everyone had eaten, Miss Rabbit
taught the children how to "swance".
"It's swimming and dancing at the same time!"
yelled Miss Rabbit over the music,
frantically waving her arms around.
"Follow me: *Swim, swim! Big fish, little fish . . .*"

"Being a mermaid is AMAZING, Daddy!" cried Peppa. "Can we have another under-the-sea party next week?"

"We'll *sea*, Peppa!" joked Daddy Pig, as he "swanced" around the room. "Being a mermaid is a lot of fun!"